Even if you have never visited California, you have probably seen Yosemite National Park. Photographs of Yosemite decorate countless calendars, postcards, and picture books. My first visit to the park came after reading about it in books and magazines, and hearing about it from adventurers, lecturers, and friends. My traveling companion, Mike, had hiked Yosemite before. As we planned our adventure, I noticed he had a twinkle in his eye. It seemed as if he knew something I didn't.

After half an hour, we entered a long, dark tunnel. The air in the tunnel was cool, calm, and damp. When we emerged, I felt as though I had been transported to another world. Yosemite Valley stretched before us, protected on all sides by sheer rock walls. The valley floor was carpeted with green grasses and trees. The enormous rocks stood cold and gray. In places, water tumbled over the valley's edge and plummeted to the valley floor. The water collected in the Merced River, the ribbon of water that weaved across the valley floor.

It was a typical summer afternoon in California. The sky was blue, the sun was shining, and people were everywhere. Some were old, many were young, and most were in between. Fat people, skinny people, tall people, and short people.

Some sat in silence. Others screamed, argued, or whispered. Cars were parked every which way, strewn about like oddities of nature. Some streaked at uncomfortable speeds past the silent, immovable rocks.

Wanting to escape the crowds, we rented a raft and floated down the Merced River. The float was slow and casual—a welcome change from the bustling streets. We stretched out on our rubber raft, trying not to touch the ice-cold water. Every bend in the river brought new beaches and trees, but the towering rocks remained always in view. We could see Yosemite Falls during most of the float. El Captain, the largest granite monolith in the world, watched over us constantly. At the opposite end of the valley, Half Dome loomed above the river.

The story of Yosemite's unique landscape began long ago. About 500 million years ago, Yosemite looked nothing like it does today. There were no towering rocks or cascading waterfalls. In fact, there wasn't even a mountain range. The Sierra Nevada region was flooded by an ancient sea. Gradually, the sea floor folded and twisted and rose above the water. At the same time, molten rock bubbled up from deep within the earth. The rock slowly cooled into hard slabs of granite.

Still, Yosemite's scenery was in the making. Layers of soft, sedimentary rock covered the granite that is visible today. Over millions of years, wind and rain wore away this overlying rock and exposed the granite. Meanwhile, the Merced River began to carve a V-shaped valley into the rocky terrain.

Eventually, the climate in the Sierra Nevadas cooled. Snow and ice blanketed much of Yosemite. In the valley and else-where, the ice flowed downhill. These massive rivers of ice, called *glaciers*, carved deep into the land. When the ice melted, Yosemite's steep-sided valley was finally revealed.

The sun was sinking close to the horizon when our raft trip ended. We joined the other tourists in a dash to claim one of the remaining campsites. We found a resting spot near some stray boulders, perhaps dropped by an ancient glacier. We were asleep almost as soon as our heads hit the ground.

When we woke the next morning, the blue skies of summer were gone. Thick, gray clouds hung just above the

ground. A slow drizzle was beginning to fall, but we couldn't complain. All around us trees, grasses, and flowers were soaking up the life-giving water. We donned our rain ponchos and headed toward Mariposa Grove.

In the Sierra Nevadas, you are always surrounded by tall, stately conifers. But in Mariposa Grove, these impressive trees are overshadowed by the grandest tree of them all—the mighty sequoia. Sequoias are the largest of all living things. Any other tree looks small next to these mammoth plants. The largest sequoia in Yosemite is named *The Grizzly Giant*. It towers more than 200 feet above the ground. It would take about 40 strides to walk around The Grizzly Giant's trunk!

turned back, the moon was rising in the east. Above the opposite horizon, Venus and Mars glowed against the twilight sky. Soon moonlight poured through the trees around us. It was a disappointment that we reached our campsite so quickly.

The next morning greeted us with blue skies and cottonball clouds. We decided to hike to the top of Half Dome, one of the enormous granite slabs that tower over Yosemite Valley. A park ranger warned us of the trail's length and steepness. She also mentioned the treacherous cables that finish the trail. We didn't take her warnings lightly. We prepared ourselves for a long and strenuous hike.

The trail began with a steep ascent, climbing over rocks that were set up like big steps. The rocks were dripping wet,